D1314731

Originally published as *Oei! Stapje voor stapje* in Belgium and the Netherlands
by Clavis Uitgeverij, 2019
English translation from the Dutch by Clavis Publishing Inc., New York

Visit us on the Web at www.clavis-publishing.com.

Oops! written by and illustrated by Mack van Gageldonk

ISBN 978-1-60537-529-8

This book was printed in November 2019 at Wai Man Book Binding (China) Ltd. Flat A, 9/F.,
Phase 1, Kwun Tong Industrial Centre, 472-484 Kwun Tong Road, Kwun Tong, Kowloon, H.K.

First Edition
10 9 8 7 6 5 4 3 2 1

Oops!

Clavis

NEW YORK

Mack

The little **mountain goat** sees a big rock.
He wants to climb up.

The little goat climbs one step at a time.

But then . . .

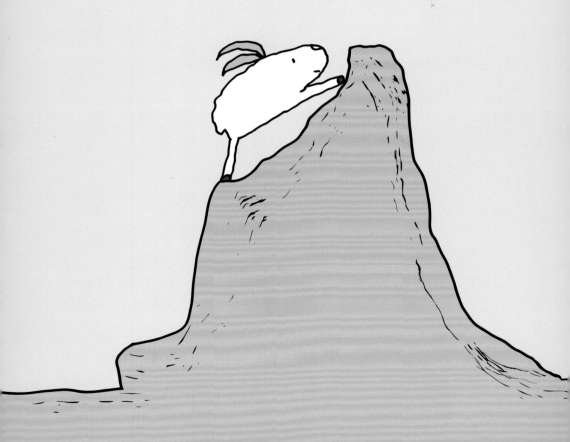

See the baby **rabbits** hop across the meadow?

Hop, hop! The rabbits move quickly.

Until . . .

The little **squirrel** is ready for a jump.

He takes off and . . .
flies through the sky to the other branch.

But then . . .

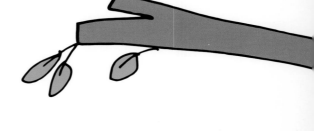

Oops!

These young **hippos** were just born,
and they are ready to take a walk.

They stomp up the hill step by step.

Until . . .

Oops!

The little **horse** sees a big fence.
He would like to jump over it.

He takes a big leap.

But then . . .

The little **monkey** is hanging high up in the trees.

He swings from one branch to another.

Until . . .

The baby **giraffe** has long legs.

They help him take big steps over the mud puddles.

But then . . .

Oops!

These **ducklings** carefully step in the water.

Can they swim?
Of course! Ducklings are great swimmers.

Until . . .

Oops!

The young **kitten** climbs high in a tree.

Oh, look! There is a bird.
The kitten tries to get a little closer.

But then . . .

Oops!

The little **bear** follows the butterflies across the water.

Step by step the little bear moves
from one stone to another.

Until . . .

The baby **goat** is hungry.

Yum! Maybe he can climb up to eat some hay.
One step at a time the little goat
climbs higher and higher.

Until . . .

These baby **penguins** totter over the ice.

Careful now. The ice can be slippery.

Almost there . . .

The baby **elephant** is so proud of his long trunk.

Cheerfully he takes his first steps.

Until . . .

Oops!

New adventures are exciting,
even if you fall
every now and then,
because . . .

. . . there is always a friend
to pick you up and give you
a sweet little kiss.